Text copyright © 2013 Daniel Cleary
Illustration copyright © 2013 Kanako Usui
Balloon Toons® is a registered
trademark of Harriet Ziefert, Inc.
All rights reserved/CIP data is available.
Published in the United States 2013 by
🍎 Blue Apple Books
515 Valley Street, Maplewood, NJ 07040
www.blueapplebooks.com

First Edition
Printed in China 04/13
ISBN: 978-1-60905-295-9
2 4 6 8 10 9 7 5 3 1

BALLOON TOONS

# My Friend FRED the Plant

by Daniel Cleary

illustrated by Kanako Usui

BLUE APPLE

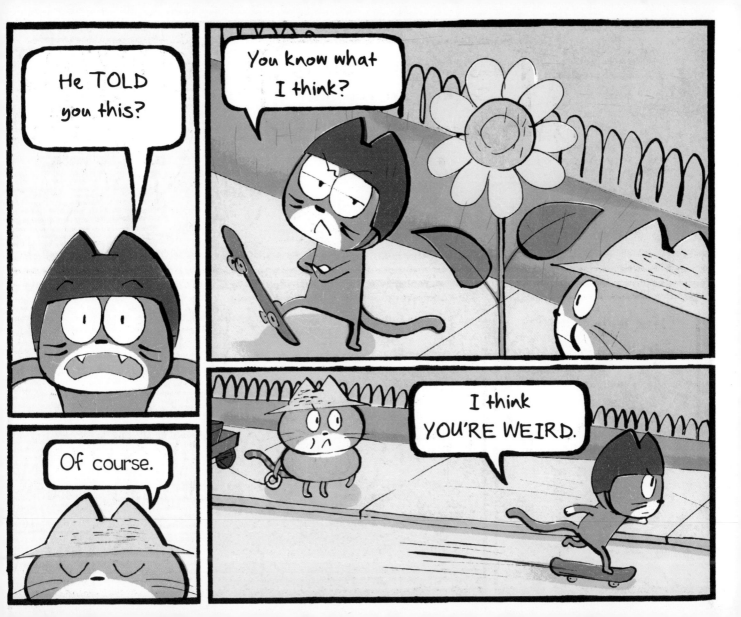

Here you go Fred.

You can let go now.